# CAMILA
## THE SOCCER STAR

written by *ALICIA SALAZAR*

illustrated by *MÁRIO GUSHIKEN*

cover artwork by *THAIS DAMIÃO*

PICTURE WINDOW BOOKS
a capstone imprint

Published by Picture Window Books, an imprint of Capstone
1710 Roe Crest Drive, North Mankato, Minnesota 56003
capstonepub.com

Library of Congress Cataloging-in-Publication Data
Names: Salazar, Alicia, 1973- author. | Gushiken, Mário, illustrator. |
Damião, Thais, artist.
Title: Camila the soccer star / written by Alicia Salazar ; illustrated by
Mário Gushiken ; cover artwork by Thais Damião.
Description: North Mankato, Minnesota : Picture Window Books, an
imprint of Capstone, 2023. | Series: Camila the star | Audience: Ages 5-7. |
Audience: Grades K-1. | Summary: Camila's soccer team, Las Estrellas Fugaz,
has lost three games in a row, so the players get together to practice working
as a team, which they hope will turn their season around. Includes glossary
and discussion points.
Identifiers: LCCN 2022028991 (print) | LCCN 2022028992 (ebook) |
ISBN 9781484671115 (hardcover) | ISBN 9781484671078 (paperback) |
ISBN 9781484671085 (pdf) | ISBN 9781484671146 (kindle edition)
Subjects: LCSH: Hispanic American girls—Juvenile fiction. | Soccer stories. |
Teamwork (Sports)—Juvenile fiction. | CYAC: Soccer—Fiction. | Teamwork
(Sports)—Fiction. | Hispanic Americans—Fiction.
Classification: LCC PZ7.1.S2483 Cav 2023 (print) | LCC PZ7.1.S2483 (ebook) |
DDC 813.6 [E]—dc23/eng/20220712
LC record available at https://lccn.loc.gov/2022028991
LC ebook record available at https://lccn.loc.gov/2022028992

Designer: Hilary Wacholz

Printed and bound in the USA. P0518S

# TABLE OF CONTENTS

# Meet Camila and Her Family

Papá

Mamá

Ana, age 14

Andres, age 10

Camila, age 7

# Spanish Glossary

**divertido** (dee-ver-TEE-doh)—fun

**fútbol** (FOOT-bohl)—soccer

**juntos** (HOON-toh)—together

**Las Estrellas Fugaz** (LAHS ehs-TREH-yas foo-GAHS)—the shooting stars

**Mamá** (mah-MAH)—Mom

**Papá** (pah-PAH)—Dad

**partido** (par-TEE-doh)—game

# Chapter 1
# A CONSTELLATION

Camila burst into her family's living room. "I'm on the **fútbol** team!" she yelled.

"She made three goals at practice," said **Mamá**.

"Coach Russo thinks I would be a great forward," said Camila. She showed off her dribbling moves.

"Not in the house," said **Mamá**.

"What is your team name?" asked Ana.

"**Las Estrellas Fugaz**," said Camila.

"The Shooting Stars," said Andres. "That is perfect for you."

"I'm part of a constellation now," said Camila. "A whole group of stars!"

"I have to go practice some more," said Camila.

"But first, homework," said **Papá**.

Camila did her homework, but she thought about soccer moves.

Juggling, kicking, passing. She practiced them all in her mind.

The first **partido** was a week away. Camila had to be ready. She worked with her team. Practice was tough. Every muscle hurt.

The day of the first game came and . . .

*Gooooooaaal!*

For the other team.

Las Estrellas Fugaz lost the first game to the Goalbusters.

They lost their second game to the Cyclones.

And the third game to the Wolf Pack.

# Chapter 2

# WORKING TOGETHER

Las Estrellas Fugaz were crushed. They sat on the grass after their third loss.

"I'm good at kicking," said Camila. "But I can't dribble very well."

"I'm good at juggling," said Kai. "But I need to work on passing."

"I'm fast," said Mya. "But I can never stay in position."

"I'm good at stealing," said Levi. "But I always go to the wrong place when you guys have the ball."

"That doesn't mean we are bad at soccer," said Camila. "That just means we need to practice working **juntos**."

"Exactly," said Mya. "We can invite all the players."

"Let's look for soccer drills on the computer," said Camila. "We can each find an activity to practice together."

"A *fun* activity," said Mya.

Feeling brighter than before, they high-fived each other and went home.

On Monday each team member dribbled a ball. They weaved between cones.

On Wednesday, the team practiced long kicks by playing keep away.

On Friday, the team pretended parts of the field was lava. They helped each other across.

"Can we do that every day?" Levi said, laughing.

"I know, right?" said Camila. "It's so **divertido**!"

# Chapter 3
# GOOOOAL!

Official practices were on Tuesday and Thursday.

On Saturday, **Las Estrellas Fugaz** were ready.

"Kick the ball. Take the shot. Come on, Team. Give it all you've got!" they cheered.

They got into position.

# They dribbled.

They passed.

They kicked . . .

And *GOOOOAAL!*

Las Estrellas Fugaz scored!

They did it. They worked
together. And they made
another goal.

And another one.

Las Estrellas Fugaz won the game!

"We are stars," said Levi.

"If we keep working together, we can win the Gold Cup," said Mya.

"We will," said Camila.
"But for now, I love being
part of our constellation."

# Soccer Simon Says

Las Estrellas Fugaz used drills and games to get better at their soccer skills. Here is a soccer game you can play with your friends to practice or just for fun! All you need is a soccer ball and at least four people to play.

## WHAT YOU DO

1. Choose one player to be Simon. This player will face the others and give commands. The commands should be soccer-related actions. See the next page for some ideas.

2. If Simon starts the command by saying "Simon says," everyone should do the action. If Simon doesn't say "Simon says" first, the players should stay still.

3. If anyone moves when "Simon says" has not been said, they are out and must sit down. The last person standing wins and is Simon for the next round.

## SOCCER SIMON SAYS COMMANDS

- Kick with only your left foot.
- Juggle the ball.
- Change direction.
- Trade balls by kicking to a partner.
- Kick then quickly stop the ball.

# Glossary

**activity** (ak-TIV-uh-tee)—a game or exercise that teaches something

**constellation** (kahn-stuh-LAY-shuh)—a group of stars that forms a shape

**dribble** (DRIH-buhl)—to move the ball along by kicking it with your feet

**forward** (FOR-wurd)—a player whose main job is to score goals

**juggle** (JUG-guhl)—to keep the ball off the ground using any part of the body except the hands and arms

**muscle** (MUHSS-uhl)—a body part that helps you move, lift, or push

**weave** (WEEV)—to move back and forth or from side to side

# Think About the Story

1. After reading the story, what do you think it takes to be a soccer star?

2. Do you play soccer? If so, what are some of your favorite things about the sport? If not, does this story make you want to try it? Why or why not?

3. Have you ever lost a game? Compare how you felt after a loss to how Las Estrellas Fugaz felt after their losing streak. What about winning? How does it feel to win a game?

4. Create a team name for a soccer team. Write it at the top of a sheet of paper. Then draw a picture of yourself wearing a soccer jersey you've designed just for your team.

## About the Author

Alicia Salazar is a Mexican American children's book author who has written for blogs, magazines, and educational publishers. She was also once an elementary school teacher and a marine biologist. She currently lives in the suburbs of Houston, Texas, but is a city girl at heart. When Alicia is not dreaming up new adventures to experience, she is turning her adventures into stories for kids.

## About the Illustrator

Mário Gushiken has been working as an illustrator since 2014. While he currently works mainly on book publishing projects, he has worked in the editorial, animation, advertising, and fashion industries. In his spare time, Mario likes to hang out with friends and play video games.